Contents

DOCTOR DEATH

DOCTOR DEATH

Edgar J. Hyde

CCP

Chapter 1

Sporting Hero

Ever gone to visit the doctor but felt worse afterwards instead of better? Well, that's just what happened to Josh Stevens and a few of his best mates when *Dr Death*, as he quickly became known, came to practise in their town. Let me tell you what happened . . .

"Go, Josh!" Simon yelled to his best mate as he passed him, changing pace slightly, to bounce the ball in Josh's direction. Josh caught the ball as it bounced back up, ducking out of the way of the Merton Vale defence. He jumped, aiming straight for the basketball net. Almost in slow motion, as everyone in the gym sucked in their breath, the ball gently circled the rim of the net. Josh could see, from the corner of his eye, Coach Barnes get up from the bench and

stand, staring at the ball, almost willing it to drop through the net. It worked, or at least something did, for the next minute it seemed as though the entire school erupted as the ball finally stopped circling and fell straight through the basket. They had won. Their team had beaten Merton Vale for the first time in seven years and Josh had scored the winning basket! Simon and the rest of the team whooped gloriously, punching the air in delighted victory, everyone grinning from ear to ear.

"Brilliant, Josh, just brilliant." Coach Barnes slapped Josh on the back. "Had us on the edge of our seats there, though. Thought the final whistle was going to blow before you scored. Well done, Josh, well done!"

As the losing team left to commiser-
ate with each other in the shower room,
the boys revelled in their victory. Everyone in the gym remained standing, ap-
plauding the first team to bring back the
cup in so many years. Grabbed from behind, Josh was hoisted aloft on his team
mates' shoulders. They carried him
around on their lap of honour singing
"For he's a jolly good fellow" at the tops
of their voices – and Josh loved it. Every
minute of it. He had never felt so special
in all his life, and he was determined to
savour every moment. He played to the
crowd, waving and smiling to them, not
caring that his hair was stuck to his head
and his face scarlet and dripping with
perspiration. As they began on their second lap of honour, Josh noticed Karen

with some of her friends. Karen Summers, the love of his life, and she had just witnessed his moment of glory, his five minutes of fame. Josh gave her a special smile as he passed by. She just *had* to go out with him now. How could she refuse to go out with the High School hero? All Josh had to do was pluck up the courage and ask her, and he'd have a date for Saturday night with the best looking girl in school.

The team stopped at the far end of the pitch and the boys lowered Josh to the ground. Still euphoric, but calmer now, they stood proudly alongside the Coach while the Headmaster, Mr Jenkins, pinned on their winners' medals.

"Well done, son," he congratulated Josh. "It's a proud day for us all."

He moved on to the next boy in line and Josh glanced up at Coach Barnes. He winked at Josh and nodded his head slowly, in the way someone does when they're glad about what you've just done. Josh smiled back, straightened his shoulders and puffed out his chest with pride. He wanted the moment to go on and on forever.

Later, in the showers, there were lots of high jinks as they all good naturedly splashed one another. Smelly tee-shirts, shorts and trainers thrown into sports bags, the friends walked out of the school gates and started to make their way home. Every second of the game was dissected, discussed and looked at from every angle. Every goal they'd scored was exaggerated, with players jumping higher, dribbling faster and scoring much easier than any other team they'd ever seen. In conclusion, though this was far from the truth, for the other team were more than worthy opponents, the boys decided the other team needn't have been there at all, so great were the circles they had run around them.

As the boys neared home, so the animated little band grew smaller.

"Bye Kev – see you tomorrow," shouted Simon as Kevin left them to cross the road to his house.

In answer, Kevin raised his arm in a victory salute and ran happily up his front pathway.

"See you guys," said Charlie, bending to tie his shoe lace.

"See you, Charlie," Josh returned as

Simon and he continued their walk.

"Did you see Karen Summers?" Josh asked as he turned to look at his best friend.

"I sure did," Simon replied. "How could I miss her? She was the one who cheered loudest when you scored the winner."

"She was?" Josh asked, looking at his friend to see whether or not he was joking, but his face remained impassive.

"Look, Josh," he stopped and turned to face him. "You've got to ask the girl for a date. I mean everyone knows you're mad about her, everyone except her that is. I'm telling you, if you don't move quickly someone else is going to snap her up right from under your nose. That girl's too pretty by far to be left on her own for any length of time."

"I know, Simon," Josh sighed. "But what if she says no?"

Having just resumed walking, Simon stopped again. "Josh, man, are you kidding me? Look, how many times have we gone over this – you're an okay guy, Josh, I never saw any reason before why she shouldn't go out with you, but now, after today?" In a rare show of affection, or perhaps it was sheer exasperation, Simon punched his friend on the shoulder. "Go for it kid," he smiled. "Hey, what's the worst thing that can happen?"

Josh smiled back, wishing he felt as confident as Simon looked. They had stopped just outside Josh's gate. He undid the latch and said goodbye to his friend. "Thanks, Si, see you tomorrow.

And remember, Thornton High are the best." They gave each other a "high five" (too many American sitcoms) and Josh pushed open his front door.

Chapter 2

A Spot of Bother

"It's me, Mum" he shouted, dropping his sports bag in the hall. "Guess what?" he went on as he headed for the kitchen. "We won the cup – first time in seven years – and guess who scored the winning goal?"

He heard Mum start to come down the stairs as he took a can of coke from the fridge.

"Josh – is that you?" she began. "I hope you haven't left dirty sports gear in your bag – put it in the washing machine if you want it washed. You kids seem to think clean clothes appear magically in your drawers having spent a couple of days lying on the floor. Never seem to think of washing machines, tumble dryers and irons, do you?"

Josh took a bite from a Snickers bar and

didn't bother to answer. He didn't need to – his mother answered all her own questions anyway. Carrying the offending sports bag, his mum entered the kitchen.

"What's this, then?" she asked, waving the bag around in front of Josh's face. "Dirty sports gear, that's what" she said.

See! The mother who answered all her own questions! Josh turned to look at his mum, vaguely curious to know if he would be allowed to answer anything she asked him today.

"And what's that you're eating? Chocolate! You'll never be able to eat dinner, Josh. I don't know why you have to snack between meals. Don't they give you enough to eat at school? Oh, I know, don't tell me, you didn't fancy what was on the menu so you and Simon went to the baker's and had a snack."

She actually looked at her son at that point for confirmation. Unfortunately, Josh had too much chocolate in his mouth to answer in the positive or negative, so he just had to let her carry on. Filling up the little plastic ball with washing powder, she turned the dial on the washing machine and clicked the switch to 'on'. Straightening up, she spotted the half empty coke in Josh's hand.

"Josh!" she admonished. "When will you ever learn? Chocolate *and* fizzy drinks! Your spots will never clear up if you don't stop eating so much junk food."

"I know, Mum," Josh said, draining what was left of the coke. "But somehow a piece of fruit and a glass of water just don't hold the same attraction, you know?"

The washing machine had started its cycle and Josh walked upstairs to change out of his school clothes. "I wonder why that little plastic ball never melts?" he wondered as he reached the top of the stairs.

"Josh," mum shouted after him. "Did you hear what I said? I'm taking you to see our new doctor tomorrow – Dr Blair, I think his name is – to see if he can do anything to help your skin. I'll pick you up straight after school, okay? And don't, for Heaven's sake, tell him you pig out on chocolate bars and cans of coke. Let me do the talking, if you don't mind."

"Let *me* do the talking," Josh thought to himself. Just who was she kidding –

with his mother around no-one else ever got the chance to do *any* talking, least of all him. He flopped on top of his bed and stretched over to reach the little hand mirror on his bedside table. His spots were a lot better, he thought, as he examined himself in the mirror. Sure, his forehead could look quite bad, but if he just kept his hair that little bit longer, and remembered to brush it in a certain way, it practically covered his spots over. Still, it wouldn't do any harm to see this new guy – maybe he could come up with something old Dr Feldman hadn't known about. The old man had retired from practice, a lot later than he should have, according to his mum, and this new guy must be the one who had taken his place. "Dr Blair, eh?" he thought to himself. "Well, then, let's see if you know your stuff."

Chapter 3

Doctor Popular

Next day Charlie wasn't at school.

"His mum said he had a – now, how was it she put it?" Kevin laughed. "Oh yes, an 'upset tummy' he finished, doing a passable imitation of Charlie's mum's voice. "When I called for him this morning that's what she said. Not 'sorry, Kev, he can't get off the toilet seat', or 'sorry, Kev, he has a bad case of the runs', just 'sorry, Kev, he has an upset tummy – too much excitement yesterday probably'." Josh and Simon laughed too, thinking of all the fun they'd have when Charlie got back to school, making loud wind noises in class, putting loo rolls in his school bag, etc.

Josh sat on his own during his geography period, as it was the absent Charlie who normally sat beside him in this class.

He didn't mind one bit though, for he spent the whole of the class staring at the back of Karen Summers' head. He had chosen this seat especially at the start of term. It was the only class he shared with Karen and he had been determined he should sit close by her for at least half an hour twice a week. As the bell rang to signify the end of the period, she stood up to gather her books together. She turned to Josh.

"Congratulations, Josh. You played brilliantly yesterday – you must be really proud." She smiled, and waited to see what Josh would say.

"Gee, thanks," he muttered, rising to his feet. Self consciously he tugged at his hair, pulling it forward to hide the horrible spots on his forehead. As he stood up, he knocked over his chair, which in turn knocked over the chair behind him, then knocked against the desk. "Sorry, sorry," he stammered, blushing furiously and turning to help whoever he'd knocked over behind him. The desk and chair were empty, a fact he'd been well aware of earlier, but had merely confused by his embarrassment. Righting both desk and chair, he coughed to cover his unease and turned back to Karen, trying desperately to think of something smart and funny to say. She'd gone. He was practically the last one left in the classroom, apart from that pathetic little swot Jones, who was always at the front of the class, asking the teachers one thing or another, and Karen, beautiful, perfect Karen, had gone.

Sighing heavily, he picked up his

books and left the classroom. He could kick himself. What an idiot! The chance of a lifetime and he'd blown it. He'd better not tell Simon, or he'd go berserk – and after all wasn't he entitled to! Friday afternoon – second last period – and he blew what could have been his first Saturday night date with Karen! He had no idea what his history teacher spoke about for the next period as he remonstrated with himself over and over again. Finally, after what seemed an age, the bell rang and he was able to leave school. As he came through the outer doors, he was surprised to see his mother's car parked outside. She tooted noisily and signalled at him to hurry up. He'd forgotten. The doctor's appointment. Though he may as well be covered in spots from head to toe considering the way he'd just behaved with Karen. Great huge boils, he thought, as he crossed the road. With a few white heads and some large green ones oozing with pus, just for good measure. Whole face may as well be one huge spot, for that matter, with green *and* yellow poison seeping from it.

"Hi, Mum," he said as he opened the car door. Checking her mirror and putting the car into gear, Mrs Stevens pulled away.

"Hi yourself," she smiled. "And what's made you so unhappy on this fine day?"

Josh shrugged and looked out of the window.

"I was talking to Charlie's mum today. You didn't tell me your team won the basketball trophy yesterday, or that you scored the winning goal?"

"I did, Mum" Josh began. "You just weren't listening . . ."

"I said to Marjorie this morning, now isn't that just typical of my son. Never tells me anything that may be important – spends all his time out of school holed up in his room, making occasional forages to the fridge. Marjorie said herself she probably wouldn't have known either, only Charlie wasn't himself last night, an upset tummy she said, and apparently that's how he gets when he's been over-excited. She said you all got medals and that it was the first time you had the won the cup in – how many years? Oh yes, seven that's right."

Josh raised his eyes heavenwards then

resumed looking out of the window. He wondered briefly if Karen was capable of droning on like this. Horrified, he shut the thought out very quickly. No, he decided, this trait was exclusive to only his mother, surely, this was simply his mum being his mum.

Arriving at the surgery, neither Josh nor his mum could believe their eyes. The car park was filled to capacity, and there were cars double parked on either side of the road.

"Good Heavens," Mrs Stevens breathed as she circled the car park for the third time, "there must be some sort of epidemic. I've never seen the surgery so busy in all my life."

Josh had to agree – even the annual summer fare held in the school grounds didn't attract as many people as this – he wondered what on earth was going on.

"Look mum – over there," he pointed.

"Oh yes, dear, well spotted," Mrs Winterman from the bakery had just come out of the surgery and was getting ready to reverse her car out of the car park. "I wonder what's wrong with her?" Mrs Stevens thought aloud. "She doesn't *look* ill, I have to say."

Josh and his mum were dumbfounded when they pushed open the door of the surgery. There wasn't a seat to be had in the place, mothers with toddlers squirming on their laps were seated beside young girls with new babies who in turn sat beside elderly arthritic ladies who clutched their walking sticks to their sides.

The normally composed receptionist was rushed off her feet, the phone was ringing off the hook, buzzers buzzing and people continuously demanded appointments. As Mrs Stevens and Josh approached the desk the receptionist was finishing a call.

"Yes, that's fine, Mrs Collins, two weeks on Monday at 9.30 am." She searched frantically for her pen. Josh pointed to behind his ear and she looked at him quizzically. She lifted the appointments book and looked underneath that before checking in her pocket. Josh again tapped the side of his head, just above his ear.

"Sorry, Mrs Collins, just a moment, I seem to have mislaid my pen." She touched her hand to the side of her head and at once located the missing object. Smiling her thanks to Josh, she wrote in the appointment, said goodbye to her caller and replaced the handset. Pushing her hair back from her eyes, she looked expectantly at Mrs Stevens.

"Oh . . . Josh Stevens," said his mum. "We have an appointment with Dr Blair at 4.30."

The buzzer buzzed. The receptionist checked her book then leant forward to shout through the glass partition.

"Mrs Burns, Dr Blair will see you now." She watched Mrs Burns make her way into the doctor's room then turned back towards Josh.

"I'm afraid we're running a little behind schedule. We've just been so busy, as I'm sure you can see, but if you'd like to take a seat, if you can find one, that is, I'm sure the doctor shouldn't be too long."

Josh was about to say they'd come back some other day, but his mother obviously fancied sitting there for hours and hours reading out of date magazines because she merely smiled, thanked the receptionist and went off in search of a seat.

Josh had never been so bored in his whole life. He'd spent the first 15 minutes of his wait trying not to breathe the same air as the twins who sat on his right hand side. They looked as if they had a bad case of chickenpox, and Josh certainly didn't want to be afflicted with that! He had more than enough spots to contend with! After that, he tried to work out on average whether he'd eaten more Snickers or Mars Bars this week. (He was learning all about averages in his maths class just now, and tended to practice the theory on just about everything, including how many visits he paid to the loo in a period of one week!). It was no use, though, he couldn't remember whether he'd had a Mars on Wednesday or if that had been the day he'd deviated altogether and had a Galaxy.

He glanced at his mum and wondered if it was worthwhile suggesting they leave. She was chewing her left thumbnail, the way she always did when she was concentrating on something. Leaning closer, Josh was able to see she was immersed in an article entitled "Does your Partner <u>Really</u> Listen?" No point in suggesting leaving then. He sighed, shifting uncomfortably in his seat. It was getting hot in here now, too. He pulled at the neck of his sweatshirt. He'd have to take his jacket off soon.

"Don't fidget, Josh," his mum said absent mindedly, never taking her eyes from her magazine.

"Mrs Stevens," called the red-faced, harassed receptionist. "Mrs Stevens, Dr Blair will see you now."

"Oh, right," his mum sat up with a jolt, her front teeth going right through her thumbnail as she did so. "Blast," she murmured involuntarily then, straightening her skirt, she smiled apologetically at the people she pushed past and, with Josh just behind, she entered Dr Blair's room.

Chapter 4

Doctor Perfect?

"Mrs Stevens, how nice to meet you." Dr Blair got up and walked towards them, his hand outstretched towards Josh's mum. "And you must be Josh," he smiled at the boy, still holding onto Mrs Stevens' hand. Josh looked at his mother, noting that she didn't seem to be trying too hard to disentangle herself from the doctor's grasp.

"Please, take a seat," the doctor continued, as he finally let go of Mrs Steven's hand and closed the door.

Barbara Stevens was gobsmacked. Now she knew why the waiting room was crammed full of females. This guy was drop-dead gorgeous! At least 6 feet 2, a shock of unruly dark hair, and the most piercing blue eyes she'd ever had the pleasure of looking into.

Josh nudged her sharply with his elbow.

"What? Oh, sorry, Dr Blair – did you ask me something?"

Shifting in her seat, Mrs Stevens cleared her throat and tried to concentrate on what the doctor was saying, instead of staring into his deep blue eyes.

Dr Blair smiled, a slow lazy smile which lit up his whole face. Eyes twinkling, he picked up his pen before opening Josh's file.

"What exactly can I help you with today?" he repeated, looking from Mrs Stevens to Josh, then back again to Mrs Stevens.

Gathering her composure, Mrs Stevens leaned over Josh and pushed his hair back from his face.

"It's his skin, Dr Blair. Spots, you see, lots of them."

"There aren't that many, Mum" Josh flushed, embarrassed.

Ignoring him, Mum went on. "They can get a lot worse than this, and sometimes his whole face is affected. I just wondered if there was any cream you would recommend he should use, other than the one he has at present. He can be a bit sensitive, you know, at his age, starting to get interested in girls, though he pretends otherwise, don't you Josh?"

She smiled and winked at Josh, as though they shared some sort of special secret. That was it. The ultimate embarrassment. Josh wanted to die. First of all his mother going all silly over the new doctor, then having to sit there while she exposed all his spots, and now telling this stranger that he was into girls! Josh flushed to his roots, knowing as he did so that it only made his spots stand out all the more, red angry pimples all clustered together on his forehead.

Dr Blair got up and came over for a closer look, though Josh thought he could have seen perfectly well from the other side of his desk, so big did he think his spots now appeared. He bent and peered closely at the mortified boy's forehead.

"Ah, yes" he mumbled. "Just a mild form of acne. Nothing we can't deal with here."

Acne! thought Josh. Acne! Old Doc Feldman hadn't said it was acne! Just some teenage spots, he'd said. Not acne! How terrible! He couldn't tell his pals about this! What if Karen got to find out? She'd never go out with a boy with acne, school basketball hero or not! He'd have to keep this *very* quiet.

He turned to hear what the doctor was saying, at the same time making himself a silent promise never to snack on chocolate and fizzy drinks ever again.

"No need go to the pharmacy – I have some ointment already made up here, Mrs Stevens," Dr Blair was saying. He took a small tub of clear ointment from his drawer and placed it on the desk in front of him. "There you go, Josh. Simply rub that into the spots every night before you go to bed and you'll soon see a marked difference, I can promise you."

Mrs Stevens lifted the tub and put it into her handbag. "Thank you ever so much, Dr Blair, you've been very kind. Should we make another appointment to come back and see you, you know, just to see how he's progressing?"

She put her head on one side as she stood up, and her voice sounded silly and squeaky as she spoke. Josh wanted to be sick. His mother *fancied* the doctor! She was a complete embarrassment. She always did the "head-on-one-side-squeaky-voice bit" when she liked someone. He'd seen it all before and each time it made him cringe.

"There shouldn't be any need, I don't think," replied the doctor. "But if you feel another visit's necessary then, yes, I should be delighted to see you."

He opened the door and again shook Mrs Stevens' hand.

"It's been a real pleasure," he told her. "See you again some time."

"Thank you, Dr Blair, thank you," mum gushed as she almost tripped over a toy lying on the waiting room floor. Regaining her balance, she smiled her thanks once more and made to leave.

Anyone would think he'd just performed life saving open heart surgery on me the way she's going on, Josh thought to himself as he too left the room.

"Spots, Josh?" The doctor spoke softly. Josh turned back to look at him. "You ain't seen nothin' yet."

Then, pressing his buzzer, he asked for his next patient to be sent in.

"What did you just say?" asked Josh, who thought he must be hearing things.

His face like stone now, the twinkly

smile long gone, Dr Blair glanced briefly at the child.

"Close the door, I said. You're causing a draft."

Chapter 5

Spot the Difference

Doctor Death

Josh threw an apple core into the bin. He'd resolved firmly in his mind now that he was turning over a new leaf. No more junk food, and an ointment application every night. He was determined to rid himself once and for all of his spots, *and* determined not to pay another visit to Dr Blair's surgery ever again. Today had been the ultimate in humiliation for him, and if his mother wanted to see the good doctor again, she could go on her own. Josh certainly wouldn't be accompanying her, that was for sure. And that closing remark, now that *was* strange. Josh didn't know whether he was imagining things or not but, even if he had imagined what the doctor's parting words were, he certainly hadn't imagined the look on his face. "A complete change from when Mum was around," the boy thought as he unscrewed the lid of the tub and dipped his finger into the ointment. "Here goes, then" he told his reflection as he began rubbing the cream onto his forehead. "Over to you, Dr Blair – do your worst!"

Reaching out of bed next morning, he shut out Bart Simpson's voice on his alarm clock. He yawned sleepily and snuggled back under the covers.

"Just another ten minutes," he thought, as he did every morning, knowing full well that his mum would wake him if he didn't appear for breakfast on time. Cocooned like a caterpillar in his duvet, he allowed himself to wake slowly, letting thoughts of what today would bring creep into his head.

"Saturday," he thought happily. "Paper round, back for a huge breakfast then meet Simon and the rest of the gang for some serious hanging about down at the centre. Might even spot Karen down there, if I'm lucky. Spot!" he thought, suddenly alert. "I'd forgotten the spot cream. I wonder if it's worked yet!" Jumping out of bed with a crash, and causing his mother to "tut" from her position at the breakfast table downstairs, he rushed over to his dressing table mirror for a look. He gasped. "Holy cow – what the – I can't believe this! No, no!" he shouted. "Mum, come up here, you have to help me, Mum, come quickly, please."

Babs Stevens took the stairs two at a time. He must have fallen when she heard the crash, and she thought he'd just been mucking about as usual. Dear Lord, he'd probably cracked his head open on the bedside table.

"Josh," she flew into the room. "What is it, baby, what's wrong?" She stopped in her tracks. The boy was fine, kneeling in front of his dressing table mirror with not a scratch in sight.

"Josh Stevens," she admonished, sitting on the edge of his bed to catch her breath. "You gave me such a fright – I thought there was something wrong, that you'd fallen and hurt yourself."

"Wrong! Wrong! Of course there's something wrong! Look at my face, or what's left of my face! You know the expression can't see the wood for the trees, well try can't see the face for the spots!"

Mrs Stevens looked more closely at her

son. "Oh, yes," she agreed. "I see what you mean. There *are* a few more this morning. And what's that one on the bridge of your nose – is it green or yellow pus?"

She bent forward to touch Josh's face and he pulled away quickly.

"Don't touch them, Mum, you'll spread them even further!" He turned back to the mirror, horrified.

"A few more!" Well, if that wasn't the understatement of the century! Yesterday's cluster of red pimples had now multiplied, and it wasn't just his forehead which was affected. He had a sprinkling on either cheek, the offending one on the bridge of his nose, and the ones which had always been on his forehead had doubled in size and filled up with alternating pockets of green or yellow pus! He simply couldn't believe his eyes.

"I can't go out looking like this, mum. Young children will take fright, cats and dogs will take to their heels in terror, my mates won't want to be seen with me, and what if I see Karen!"

Horrified at the prospect of coming face to face with the girl he had eagerly looked forward to seeing just a few minutes earlier, Josh shook his head in dismay. His mother reached out to pat his shoulder comfortingly.

"Josh, Josh, calm down, come on now. It's not as bad as you think. Once you've washed your hair and dried it over your forehead the way you usually do, you won't look half so bad, honestly."

"It's that new cream" Josh said disgustedly. "I should never have listened to you and that new doctor. My skin wasn't so bad yesterday, and look at me now – I look as though I just spent four hours in make-up getting ready for a part in a Freddie Krueger movie!"

Mrs Stevens suppressed a smile and picked up the tub of cream.

"Listen, Josh" she said softly. "It says here on the side of the tub 'may make condition worse before any improvement is seen'. You see – worse before it gets better – your Gran used to say that, don't you remember?"

"Sure, I remember" Josh said huffily, "only I thought it was just another old wives' tale."

"Well, there may be some truth in this one," said mum as she replaced the tub on the dressing table. "Look, Josh, try and see the positive side of this. It's Saturday, right? You apply the cream tonight again and then you'll have the whole day Sunday to mope about the house looking spotty and feeling horrid. Then you apply the cream on Sunday night and, hey presto, Monday morning you get up for school with the clearest, most spot-free skin the world! So you have the worse days at home at the weekend and the better days back at school with your mates where it really matters."

Josh looked at her hopefully. "You really think so Mum?" You think that's what'll happen?"

"Well, it's possible, isn't it?" his mother answered, hiding her crossed fingers behind her back. "Come on, let's go, you've

got a paper round to do. And no buts!"
She put her fingers to her son's lips, stop-
ping his protests. "You do <u>not</u> look nearly
as bad as you think, Josh, and half the
world's still asleep anyway."

"Go on, go and get showered and off
you go. I'll have a huge breakfast waiting for you when you get back, so go
work up an appetite!"

Josh turned on the shower tap and
started to hum a little tune. Mum was
right. He had all weekend to get rid of
the spots, and the prospect of being rid
of them completely was almost too stag-
gering for words! Maybe he should apply the cream more often than just once
at night. Yes, that's what he'd do – he'd
apply it once every few hours just to
speed the process along. He let the hot

water run over his hair and down his back. Gosh! He could hardly wait till Monday morning.

Arriving at the shopping centre later that day, Josh was both surprised and pleased to see Charlie there with Kevin and Simon.

"Hey, Charlie" he called. "Howya doin?" Charlie turned towards his friend and smiled weakly. "Gosh, you look awful" said Josh, aghast. And he did, too. His face looked thinner, somehow, his eyes seeming to sink deep into their sockets, and his pallor was distinctly on the grey side.

"Thanks, Josh, you sure know how to make a guy feel better!"

"Sorry," said Josh. "I didn't mean to . . . it's just that you normally look . . ."

Charlie held up his hand to quieten his friend. "It's okay, Josh, really, it's cool. I know how I look. I don't feel that great, either, I have to admit, but don't tell my mum I said that – I had a hard enough job persuading her to let me come out today as it was!"

Josh and the others nodded sympathetically. They knew what their own mothers were like, after all.

"Anyway," Charlie continued, "yesterday was awful, in fact I got so bad Mum bundled me into the car last night and took me over to see the doctor, the new guy, you know, Dr Blair? So, he checks me over and gives me some sachets of stuff I have to drink three times a day. Says that should sort me out. Strangely enough, though, I've had two sachets today already and I can honestly say that I'm actually feeling worse!"

"Now that is weird," began Josh, "cos I saw Dr Blair yesterday, too. Strange guy, I thought, couldn't make my mind up whether or not I liked him, though my mum didn't seem to have the same problem."

"Oh, not yours too!" said Charlie. "I wanted to *vomit* in the nearest bucket the way my mother was carrying on. Fluffing up her hair, and pretending to be a young thing, real squirm-in-your-seat stuff".

"I know exactly what you mean," said Josh in agreement. "Sort of behaviour you'd expect from a teenager. So, anyway, this Dr Blair, he gave me some ointment to put on my spots and told me to apply it every night. Thing was, that when I woke up this morning . . ." he broke off. "Charlie – you okay?"

"I'm fine, Josh," Charlie managed to say through clenched teeth, his face contorting with pain. "I just have to get to the loo, that's all. I'll be okay."

Clutching his stomach, Charlie started to move away in the direction of the escalator which would take him to the toilets located on the lower level. Unfortunately, the guys were treated to the unwelcome stench of some gas that had escaped before Charlie moved away.

"Oh man," said Kevin, holding his nose dramatically. "Let's get out of here."

Some loud noises were emanating from Charlie's direction too as he tried to hurry to the escalator.

"We'll meet you in the Do-nut Diner," shouted Simon as the three moved away. Turning to Josh, Simon added, "though maybe your mum was right about you staying away from sugar, Josh. Your face does look a bit of a mess today."

"Cheers, Si, I can always rely on you to boost my confidence just when I really need it!"

Chapter 6

A Turn for the Worse

On Monday morning when Simon arrived at Josh's house, Josh stuck his head firmly under the covers and refused to come downstairs.

"He's still in bed, Simon," said Mrs Stevens. "Go up and see him if you like."

"Thanks, Mrs Stevens, I will," said Simon, brushing past her to go upstairs. Mrs Stevens stepped back against the wall. What on earth was that smell?

"Simon, have you trod on dog's dirt, let me check your shoes."

Simon stopped and showed the soles of both shoes. Clean. Turning his face away, he muttered. "It's not my shoes, Mrs Stevens, I only wish it was."

There it was again, that same smell. Maybe it was coming from outside. She opened the door wider to go and check and Simon took the opportunity to climb the stairs to Josh's room. Josh was still under the covers when his friend came in.

"Go away, Simon. I'm going nowhere today, or for the rest of my life for that matter. I *really* look like something out of a horror movie now."

Simon sat on the bed beside his friend.

"I know just what you mean, Josh, and believe me the best place you could be right now is underneath the covers and away from the smell of my breath!"

This statement caused Josh to move slightly, though not enough for him to stick his head out from his hiding place. His voice was muffled.

"What do you mean, Simon? What smell?"

"If I mentioned the name of Dr Blair to you, you might understand what I'm about to tell you."

More movement from under the covers.

"My mum was going to the doctor's Saturday tea-time and I went with her, mostly out of curiosity after what you and Charlie said about him. And you were right. Mr Perfect, in Mum's eyes anyway. She thought he was totally gorgeous and I think, judging by the amount of females in the waiting room, that so do half the population of the town. Anyway – he deals with Mum's problem then turns his attention to me. 'And what about you, young man – are you in perfect health, or is there anything I can help you with?' he says. So, just as I'm about to tell him fine, Mum butts in and tells him about the verruca on my foot. I mean, I've had the thing for ages, I'm treating it myself with verruca ointment and there simply isn't a problem. Between you and me, though, I think Mum just wanted to prolong the visit and spend as much time as she could drooling over this guy.

When I tell him what I've been treating my foot with, he says he has a better cure and gives me a small bottle of pills. 'Take two of these a day,' he tells me, 'and before you know it your problem will be solved.' So I did – Saturday and Sunday, then last night I started to notice it – the smell I mean." He sighed wearily. "Josh, come on, take your head out of the covers. I promise I won't laugh. I've got serious problems of my own, believe me."

Slowly, Josh sat up in his bed, revealing a face now almost completely covered in huge red, yellow and green spots. Simon let out a long low whistle.

"Wow, man, he sure did a good job on you."

Josh dived straight back under the covers.

"Hey, Simon, you weren't kidding about the smell. Can you open my window, please?"

Offended, though understanding Josh's request totally, Simon opened the window as far as it would go.

"Okay, Josh, it's open, I'll breath out this way if you want to come out again."

Josh popped his head back out of the covers.

"Go on, then," he prompted, "and explain the remark 'sure did a good job on you'. What exactly do you mean?"

"Dr Blair, Josh, that's who I mean. Don't ask me why, 'cos I don't have an explanation, but this guy's out to get us. You, me, Charlie – look at us – each one afflicted with something awful and embarrassing immediately following a visit to his surgery. My breath is so foul it's almost as though he's transferred the smell of my feet after being stuck in my trainers through a whole basketball game into my mouth. Your mum thought I'd trod on something when I came in, it's so bad."

Josh couldn't dispute that. Despite his window being opened fully, he was glad when his friend stopped talking and therefore spreading the foul smell of his breath around the room. He was grateful too soon.

"And another thing," Simon continued. "I met swotty Jones on my way over here and he was positively reeking of BO. Now a swot he may be, but he never suffered from BO before. *And* I saw him in Dr Blair's surgery on Saturday night, so if that doesn't tell you something then what does!"

Josh shook his head in disbelief. "But why, Simon? Why would a doctor want to *give* people ailments, instead of trying to cure them?"

Simon shrugged. "I don't know, Josh, it doesn't make any sense to me either. What I do know though is that our Dr Blair isn't the nice gentlemanly type he would have our mothers believe.

While they're swooning all over the place, Dr Blair here's handing out all sorts of weird potions that cause more grief than you'd care to believe. *And* he tried to shut my fingers in the door as I was leaving, only I was too quick for him."

Josh looked at his friend doubtfully. "Come on, Si, that's a bit childish isn't it? A doctor trying to shut your fingers in a door?"

"I know how it sounds, Josh," said Simon, forgetting to breath out of the window, and causing Josh to reel back against his headboard, "but I'm telling you he did. And the look on his face when I managed to get out of the way in time was not one of pleasure, I can tell you!"

Josh remembered the doctor's parting words to him on his visit to the surgery, when he thought he'd merely misheard. He repeated the words to Simon.

"'Spots – you ain't seen nothin' yet.' And, boy, was he ever right!" said Josh, snatching a quick glance at himself in the mirror. The two boys sat in silence for a few minutes, each with his own thoughts.

"Tell you what," said Josh eventually. "Mum's determined I should go to school today – who's she kidding – so let's behave as though we are going to school but go visit Dr Blair, and see if we can find out just what he's up to. I'll just grab a quick shower and we'll go."

Just as he got out of bed, his bedroom door opened and Charlie and Kevin entered. Charlie was whiter than ever and sat down very gingerly on the bed. His many visits to the loo had caused his nether regions to become somewhat "inflamed" as his mother put it. "Red raw" was closer to how Charlie would have described it.

"What's the weird smell in here?" he looked at Josh. "And it's not me – I've only just arrived."

Simon turned from the window. "I'm afraid it's me guys, and I'm afraid you're gonna have to put up with it until we can all find cures for our ailments."

"I'm just going into the shower," said Josh as he made to leave the room. "I'll leave Simon to fill you guys in on what we've been discussing." As he pushed past Kevin he stopped for a closer look. "What's that on the end of your nose, Kev, a wart?"

Self-consciously touching the new

growth at the end of his nose, Kevin nodded.

"Hay fever," he said. "That was all I went to him for – some hay fever tablets, and now look at me!"

Chapter 7

Hatching a Plan

Doctor Death

The four boys made their way to the local park, taking a long detour around the school, hoping not to be spotted by any teachers, or parents for that matter. The park keeper didn't seem to be about so they headed for the maze. Having frequented the maze for years, each of them knew exactly which way to go, and they also knew they'd be fairly safe at the centre of the maze from any unwelcome prying eyes. They sat cross-legged, Charlie grimacing as he sat down beside his friends. Where before the others would have laughed at their friend's misfortune, having been afflicted themselves they were a bit more sympathetic.

"Okay, guys," Josh began. "We have to form a plan to find out just what the good doctor's up to. And to rid ourselves of these ailments. I mean look at us – a more motley crew you'd never set eyes on. Although you look all right, Simon, you'd be fine actually if you could learn sign language and keep your mouth shut for the rest of your life."

Simon managed a wry smile. "Yeah, right, Josh. I know how bad it is. And I want it sorted out. We have to find out what this guy's up to, what sort of medicinal concoction he's given each of us, and if there's any way of reversing the process."

The boys nodded in agreement.

"Okay," said Kevin, "here's what I think we should do. "There's no point in going to the surgery just now – you know how busy it is every day. We really need to go there when the clinic's over, sneak in somehow and see exactly what's what."

"You're right," agreed Charlie. "We'll have to go later tonight when things are a bit quieter. I want to get Dr Blair back for what he's done – make him pay for all this suffering.

"That's what we'll do then," said Simon, "only if we're going to stay here all day we'll need some provisions – we're bound to get hungry."

"I'll go" said Charlie, getting to his feet. "I have to go the loo anyway, so I'll go to the shops when I'm out and buy some crisps and juice and stuff."

The boys emptied their pockets and gave Charlie what money they had.

"I hate to tell you, Kev," he said as he turned to leave, "but I think you just grew another wart on your chin!"

Having spent the day in the maze then, with poor Charlie making frequent trips in and out to the loo (and reporting sightings of children he knew sporting huge cauliflower ears they had not previously had), the four boys all dropped their school bags back home, pretending to their mothers they'd had perfectly normal days in school. They met up again at the top of the road leading to the surgery and walked in silence towards Dr Blair's practice.

The flustered receptionist was just leaving, and about to lock the outer doors, when she saw the boys approach.

"Is the doctor still inside?" Josh asked anxiously.

"Yes – he's still there – though I don't

think he'll be looking to see any more patients tonight. He's had a thoroughly exhausting day – as have I – maybe you boys could come back tomorrow?"

Simon shrugged. "It's okay, nothing that can't wait. We'll come back another time, eh guys?" he winked conspiratorially at the others.

The receptionist smiled and finished locking the main doors.

"Bye then," she said, walking towards her car.

She unlocked the door, sat down and carefully checked the sole of each shoe. "Strange," she thought to herself. "There was a strong smell of dogs' dirt back then – could have sworn I'd trod on something."

"His surgery light's still on," said

Kevin. "He's probably planning even more horrors for any kids who call on him tomorrow. We've got to find a way in there."

Circling the building, the boys couldn't believe their luck when they discovered an open window.

"Quick!" said Josh. "Help me up. I'll go in and wait till he's gone then I'll have a scout around and see if I can come up with anything. You lot stay here and see if you can find anything out from him when he leaves. Make sure he knows we're onto him – maybe if we back him into a corner he'll panic and do something stupid!

The three friends, having watched Josh climb inside the surgery, walked about outside, chatting casually, kicking empty

cans around, and generally trying to behave as normally as teenage boys do.
They walked round to the front of the
building and saw that the light was now
out in Dr Blair's surgery. The three saun-
tered over to lean against his car, looking
up casually as the doctor locked his surgery door.

"Get away from my car," he admonished them as soon as he saw them.
"Louts. Knew it the minute I set eyes on
you."

Drawing closer to the boys, he grinned
at Kevin, or at Kevin's warts.

"Working, I see" he said, obviously
pleased. "And how's Charlie – still got
the runs, my boy?" Reaching into his
pocket for his car keys he murmured almost to himself, "never lets me down,

that one, always works a treat."

"So, you're admitting it, then?" asked Simon. "You did this to us deliberately. But why? Why would you want to do such a thing."

"Oh," the doctor recoiled. "A bit too successful, that one," he said, covering his nose and taking a step backwards. "That really is the most foul smelling breath I've come across in a long time. "Won't be very popular with anyone smelling like that, Simon, will you?"

Charlie pulled at his sleeve. "You've got to give us something to counteract these effects, doctor, please – can't you see how much we're suffering?"

Dr Blair disdainfully brushed Charlie's hand from his coat sleeve.

"How dare you touch me?" he hissed

at the child. "And don't tell me I *have* to help you! Why do you think I did this, after all? I enjoy seeing your suffering – do you really think I'm going to spoil my fun and reverse the process – you can't be serious!"

"We'll tell our parents – we'll go to the police, expose you!" spluttered Kevin, enraged.

Dr Blair fixed his gaze on the boy.

"Kevin – ah yes, your mother was quite taken with me, if I remember correctly, as was yours, Simon, and yours, Charlie – do you really think they'd believe I would do anything to harm their precious children, especially afflicting them with ailments as peculiar as these? I think not, brats, but take heart – the potions will wear off in a few years." He laughed, a cold chilling laugh which hung in the air.

Turning the key in the ignition, he rolled down the window.

"Believe me, boys, I'm living proof. I used to be ugly when I was a youth, covered in all manner of pimples and warts, but just look at me now! Females who wouldn't have spared me a glance when I was a teenager are now swooning all over my surgery. Eat your hearts out, guys!" Taking his foot off the accelerator, he looked at each boy in turn. "Back off, boys, take this as a warning – I can get really nasty, and, believe me, you don't want to know about that! If I were you I'd just be grateful I had only minor afflictions, they're not exactly life-threatening – yet!" He laughed again and pressed his foot to the floor.

"Life-threatening! Life-threatening! How dare he!" exploded Kevin.

"Calm down" said Simon, patting his friend's shoulder reassuringly. "We'll sort this whole thing out, don't you worry, but we have to stay calm and try to think straight. Come on, let's go see if Josh is okay – maybe he's found something that will help us."

The three boys went around to the open window which, thankfully, the doctor had not noticed.

Chapter 8

Kill or Cure?

Meanwhile Josh, inside, had indeed found "something". He had found jars and bottles bearing labels which claimed to do things which were beyond your wildest dreams.

After he jumped down from the window, he found himself in the small kitchen where the receptionist made her now infrequent cups of coffee and stealthily made his way to the surgery.

As there was still a fair bit of sunlight streaming through the window, he was able to see things quite clearly in the room. Everything seemed normal. The doctor's desk diary showed nothing untoward, though Josh did have a hard time deciphering some of the notes scribbled there! "Typical doctor," he thought, then grinned wryly – this doctor was anything *but* typical!

The grey metal filing cabinets which lined the walls still had the keys in their locks. Josh opened the drawers easily. "Archer, Black, Dixon" he read the names from the top drawer. Pushing that drawer back in, he pulled open the middle one. "M's and Macs seemed to take up most of the space in this one, so he moved on to the bottom. "Ramsay, Smith, Stevens – that's it." He pulled out his file. "Josh Stevens" it said on the front. "Date of Birth 10.7.85'. Yeah, that was him all right – it was definitely his file. Pulling up a chair beside the doctor's desk, he opened the file and started to read. "But it's all old stuff" he thought. Like the time he had to have his knee stitched when he fell off his bike (his mum had insisted on removing his stabilisers, even though he had told her it was much too soon). And then the time he'd had an allergic reaction to a new brand of washing powder his mum had bought. Gee, that had been awful – covered in tiny little pin pricks from head to toe. He felt itchy just thinking about it! And look at that – he'd forgotten about that – the time he'd pushed one of his tiny green Lego bricks right up inside his nose and Doc Feldman had removed it with tweezers! Beginning to enjoy himself now, he leaned back in the chair and crossed his legs on the desk in front of him. He heard a noise. "What was that?" he started, sitting upright at the desk. Then he noticed. What he'd earlier assumed to be simply a wall was in actual fact sliding doors, doors which had been covered perfectly in wallpaper to conceal behind them a huge walk-in cupboard. He must have inadvertently hit the button to open the doors when he put his feet on the table. He stood up and walked towards the now exposed cupboard.

Wow! The sight that greeted him was astounding! As he walked along the right hand side of the room (for it was far more fitting that it be called a room, being much too big to be known as a cupboard), he saw more jars, bottles, tubs and every other type of container than you could ever imagine. Glancing to his left, he saw it looked almost identical. They were both shelved. The jars on the top shelf were the largest, and were filled to capacity with different coloured liquids. The containers on the second and third shelves were slightly smaller, and again filled with different colours of liquid. Concentrating on the left wall, then, Josh noticed that the bottom shelf held empty containers, in lots of different sizes, some of which were similar to the one his acne cream was in at home.

"So this is the doctor's dispensary," thought Josh, looking more closely at the jars, each of which was labelled very clearly and precisely. His eyes travelled along the top shelf. *Unbearable Itch* read the first label. *Hair Thinner* said the next. Followed by *Extremely Large and Flaky Dandruff, Chronic Diarrhoea, Foul Breath, Incontinence* (Josh shuddered when he read that one), *Stinking Armpits, Brown Stumpy Teeth, Green Pus-Filled Spots, Yellow Pus-Filled Spots, Huge Whiteheads* and, finally, *Triple Combination Spots*.

"That's it." He stopped. *"The Triple Combination* – that's what he's given me!"

Glancing further up, Josh saw a large notice above the shelves which read AF-FLICTIONS & AILMENTS. Looking to the other side of the room, he saw that the notice above those shelves read CURES & REMEDIES. The jars on the top shelf there were also labelled. Shiny, Well-Conditioned Hair, *Healthy Bowel Movements, Sweet Smelling Breath, Even White Teeth, Clear Perfect Skin.* He stopped reading and did a double take. *Clear Perfect Skin* – a dream come true! He'd check it out later – for now, though, he had to concentrate on whatever else he was able to find in the room.

Going back to the AFFLICTIONS &

AILMENTS side, he began to read the labels on the jars which lined the second shelf. *Measles, Mumps, Chickenpox, Whooping Cough* and so on.

"Bit more serious" Josh thought, shaking his head. "This Dr Blair must really be a bit of a nutter. He must have discovered, somehow, a way of 'bottling' these illnesses and then spend the rest of the time getting them into children's bodies. What a sicko!"

Looking at the corresponding shelf on the CURES & REMEDIES side of the room, he saw syringes lying beside jars which simply had the name of the illness printed on the label, with the word "vaccine" added below. More than a little anxious now, Josh was almost afraid to look at the third shelf.

He swallowed hard, and looked down. *Partial or Complete Paralysis* the first one read. Josh blanched. *Loss of Sight* said the second. Josh could feel the skin start to prickle on the back of his neck. He looked at the third. *Terminal Illness*. He knew, almost before he turned, what he would see when he looked at the corresponding right hand shelf. It was completely empty.

He heard a creaking noise. The doctor had come back and was about to catch Josh red-handed snooping about in his dispensary! He tried to flatten himself against the wall, attempting to calm down his breathing.

"Josh?" he heard. "Josh, are you in there?"

Josh exhaled deeply with relief. It was Simon – thank goodness for that.

"In here, Simon, but prepare yourself for a real shock. This guy's a real Dr Death, I'm not joking – you'll never believe what I've just found."

Simon came into the dispensary, closely followed by Kevin and Charlie. Josh indicated the notices above each wall of shelves and left the boys to read what was in each jar while he went back into the doctor's surgery to sit quietly at the desk. Simon was the first to join him, having seen all he needed to in the Chamber of Horrors next door. Neither boy spoke, waiting instead for their two friends to absorb everything they had just seen. Kevin and Charlie joined them fairly soon.

"Knew the guy was a weirdo," said Josh. "But I didn't expect to find all this stuff." Visibly shocked, his three friends could only nod. "How could anyone do such terrible things? I mean, what does he do – inject illnesses into young children then pretend to be concerned when they get really sick? And does he cure them right at the last minute or does he . . . does he simply . . ." Josh couldn't finish the sentence. It was just too awful to contemplate. The boys sat in silence, each with their own separate thoughts. "Anyone got any ideas, then?" asked Charlie. "What are we going to do?"

Standing up and pushing back his chair Josh got to his feet. "I know" he announced, looking determined. "We're going to swap the labels, that's what we're going to do. We're going to swap over the labels so that next time Dr Death prescribes *Triple Combination Spots* for someone he'll really be giving them *Clear Skin*. And next time he prescribes *Extremely Large and Flaky Dandruff*, he'll really be prescribing *Shiny Well Conditioned Hair*. Come on guys, we'd better get to work, we've got a lot to do.

"But Josh – what about the third shelf – we don't have any jars to swap with" said Charlie.

"I know, I already thought of that. One of us has to go to the supermarket, it should still be open (he checked his watch) and buy some bottles of food colouring. We'll simply empty out the contents of the jars then mix the food colouring with water and do a re-fill job. We'll just have to be really careful and make sure the doctor doesn't suspect."

Simon volunteered to go get the food colouring and, as he left by the window, checking carefully to make sure no-one saw him leave, his friends had already got down to work. They carried out the task quietly, gently removing each label and affixing it to its new home.

Before their job was complete, Josh took four small tubs and placed them carefully on the desk. Taking the larger container marked *Clear Perfect Skin*, he poured just enough to fill the first of the tubs. He replaced the large container on the shelf, then took the one marked *Sweet Smelling Breath* and filled a tub with that too. He repeated the process twice more, filling the two remaining tubs with cures for Charlie and Kevin. He screwed the lids on all four tubs, marking each with details of its contents, and put them in a bag. When Simon returned, most of the re-labelling was complete, and the boys then started to pour out the contents of the jars from the third shelf. They carefully mixed the food colouring with some water, ensuring it was just the right shade before pouring it into the appropriate jars. Eventually, everything returned to its proper place, the boys stood back and surveyed their handiwork.

"Well done, lads, good job. We'll see just how much damage Dr Death can do now!"

Leaving the dispensary, Josh once more pressed the button on the desk and closed the doors. He replaced his file in its rightful position in the filing cabinet then, lifting the bag containing the stolen cures, he and his three friends opened the window and crept out into the night.

It was darker now, and the boys had to stop under a lamp post, using its light to see the words hastily scribbled on the tops of the tubs.

"There you go, boys. I'd start taking that as soon as I got home if I were you. I know I will be, in fact I think I'll have two teaspoons before I go to bed!" said Josh.

"I think I might drink the whole tub tonight" said Simon. "Anything, anything to get rid of this odour."

Charlie and Kevin smiled and took their tubs from Josh.

"What do you think will happen?" asked Kev. "When he starts to notice that people aren't getting sick any more?"

Josh shrugged. "Who knows? It may

be that we're going to have to take this whole thing further at a later stage, but for now I think we did good."

"Yaah, you're right, Josh," agreed Charlie. "Let's go home and get some sleep – I'm bushed – and we'll get together in the morning to see how our cures are progressing."

Congratulating themselves, then, on what they had been able to do, though still anxious to know the final outcome, the weary boys said goodnight and began to make their way home.

Chapter 9

Back to Normality

"You see, what did I tell you" said Josh's mum as he came bounding downstairs next morning for breakfast. "Worse before better – your Gran and Dr Blair were both right after all."

Josh grinned, pausing again to admire himself in the mirror. His skin, though not yet completely clear, looked three quarters of the way to being cured. He still had a few red pimples on his forehead but, apart from that, he both looked and felt great.

Meeting up with the boys later that morning en route to school, he found that they too were well on their way back to normality.

"Best medicine the doctor's ever prescribed," announced Charlie.

A few hours before, Dr Blair had arrived in his surgery. He always went there early in the morning, well before his receptionist and patients, and went straight to the dispensary. After locking the door of the surgery, he removed several of the jars from the dispensary, carefully placing them in an orderly row on his desk. Then, taking a small spoon from his drawer, he unscrewed the lid of the first jar and swallowed a spoonful. He did the same with the second jar and repeated the process all the way down the line. If the boys could have seen him now, they would have laughed out loud at the sight of the good doctor readily swallowing his ailments and afflictions.

Chapter 10

Doctor Yeuch!

It was English, last period on a Friday afternoon. A month had passed since the events that took place in the surgery, and all four boys were completely cured. The sun was streaming in the classroom window as the boys listened to their teacher sum up the final scene from Macbeth. Simon pushed a note towards Josh.

"Where are you going tonight?." Josh smiled before writing "Meeting Karen at 7 and going to the cinema – will you and Cindy be there?"

Before he had time to scribble his reply, the final bell rang and both boys grabbed books and bags before running happily out of the classroom and into the summer sunshine.

The receptionist took another sip at her coffee, and turned the pages of her newspaper to the "Situations Vacant" pages. She was startled by her buzzer. She sighed.

"Yes, Dr Blair?"

"Would you bring my coffee?" he rasped.

"Certainly, doctor."

She got up from her chair and walked into the kitchen. She put some coffee and biscuits on a tray and walked towards the doctor's room. She always dreaded this part. Taking a deep breath, she knocked twice on the door, turned the handle and went in. The stench hit her as soon as she opened the door. The doctor, seated behind his desk, was barely recognisable as the smooth sophisticated Dr Blair she had originally come to work for. The man seated behind the desk was now completely bald, his eyes dull and lifeless and his once white and even teeth now reduced to brown, rotting stumps. He seemed to have shrunk in size, and appeared much thinner than he had done before. "Probably due to his frequent visits to the toilet," the receptionist thought as she placed his coffee before him. "The poor man seems to suffer from chronic bouts of diarrhoea."

He muttered his thanks and she gratefully left the room. She'd really have to find another job soon, she thought as she walked slowly back to reception through the deserted waiting room. There hadn't been a patient in here for weeks now, and who could blame them? The change in the doctor in such a short space of time was really quite unbelievable. He looked awful, he smelt awful, and he was so gruff in his manner that he frightened people away. She sat down and started to type. "Dear Sirs, I am writing in response to your recent advertisement . . .'

Dr Blair pressed the button on his desk and slowly made his way into his dispensary. He unscrewed the jar labelled *Shiny, Well Conditioned Hair* and greedily swallowed a large teaspoonful. He stopped to scratch his face, his dirty jagged nails accidentally catching the head of a spot, causing green pus to spurt from it and run down the side of his face to drip onto his collar. Lifting the jar labelled *Healthy Bowel Movements*, he wondered aloud.

"Maybe I'll have two teaspoonfuls today – maybe that would help . . ."

We hope you enjoyed this story from the pen of Edgar J. Hyde. Here are some other titles in the Creepers series for you to collect:

Blood on Tap
The Ghostly Soldier
Happy Halloween
Edgar Escapes!
Soul Harvest

This series was conceived by Edgar J Hyde and much of the text was provided by his minions under slavish conditions and pain of death! Thankfully none of the minions defied their master and so we can say 'thank you' to them for toughing it out and making this series possible.

The Ghostly Soldier

Angus and Ishbel love to hear the stories about heroic Scottish warriors. They visit the site where the Battle of Culloden was fought and Angus romanticises the events, wishing that he could have been there to help fight the Redcoats. His opinion changes when an explosion in their garden unleashes the spirits of ghostly warriors from the battle. Angus is accidentally caught up in the terrifying world of the restless spirits of English and Scottish soldiers who must fight the battle again and again. The children must return the spirits to where they belong, but how?

Soul Harvest

The Grimaldis, a creepy new family who
have a bad attitude and who dress en-
tirely in black move into Billy and Alice's
neighbourhood. Very soon afterwards
their mum and dad and all the other
neighbours start to act very strangely -
as if they have suddenly become wicked.
The children, and their friends Ricky and
Alex, are soon the only normal ones left
in a neighbourhood of thieves, bullies and
thugs. The entire village, headed by the
Grimaldi's is soon trying to find the four
children and capture their souls to make
the imminent 'harvest' complete!